For Steve
Emma Garcia

First American edition published in 2008
by Boxer Books Limited.

Distributed in the United States and Canada
by Sterling Publishing Co.,Inc.
387 Park Avenue South, New York, NY 10016-8810

First published in Great Britain in 2008
by Boxer Books Limited.

www.boxerbooks.com

Text and illustrations copyright © 2008 Emma Garcia

ISBN-13: 978-1-906250-21-8

1 3 5 7 9 10 8 6 4 2

Printed in China

All of our papers are sourced from managed forests
and renewable resources.

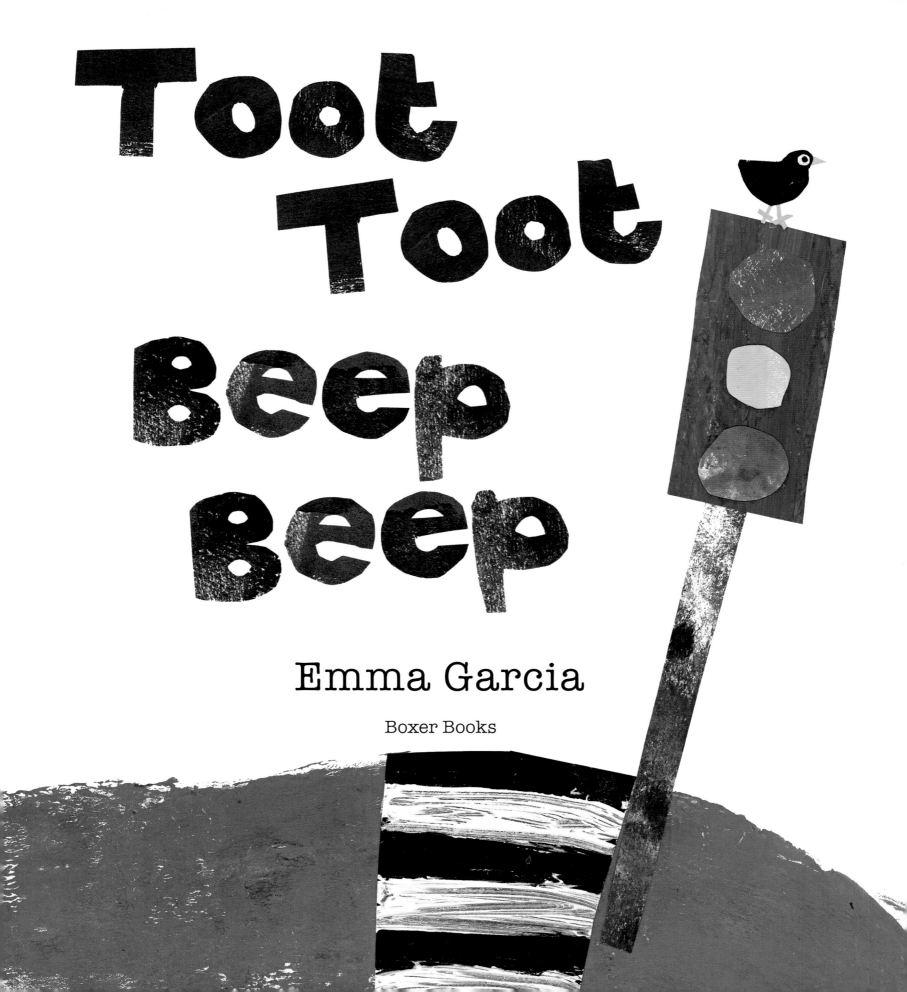

Toot Toot Beep Beep

Emma Garcia

Boxer Books

Look at all this traffic!

The cars go up and down, in and out, and round and round,

Whoosh Whoosh

Chugga Chugga

Brmm Brmm

What a lot of noise!

But wait!
It's all quiet now.
Where have all
the cars gone?

Here they all are,

in the parking lot.

Night-night, cars!